W9-ATE-586

BEGINNER BOOKS
by the Berenstains

The Bear Detectives
The Bear Scouts
The Bears' Almanac
The Bears' Christmas
The Bears' Picnic
The Bears' Vacation
The Berenstain Bears and the Missing Dinosaur Bone
The Berenstain Bears: That Stump Must Go!
The Big Honey Hunt
The Bike Lesson

BRIGHT & EARLY BOOKS
by the Berenstains

The A Book
The B Book
The C Book
Bears in the Night
Bears on Wheels
The Berenstain Bears and the Spooky Old Tree
The Berenstain Bears on the Moon
He Bear, She Bear
Inside, Outside, Upside Down
Old Hat, New Hat

The Big Honey Hunt

by Stanley and Janice Berenstain

BEGINNER BOOKS

A DIVISION OF RANDOM HOUSE, INC.

Cover art copyright © 2002 by Berenstain Enterprises, Inc.
Copyright © 1962 by Stanley and Janice Berenstain.
Copyright renewed 1990 by Stanley and Janice Berenstain.
Published in the United States by Random House Children's Books,
a division of Random House, Inc., New York,
and simultaneously in Canada by Random House of Canada Limited, Toronto.
Originally published by Random House, Inc., in 1962.
www.randomhouse.com/kids
www.berenstainbears.com
This title was originally cataloged by the Library of Congress as follows:
Berenstain, Stanley.
The big honey hunt, by Stanley and Janice Berenstain.
[New York] Beginner Books [1962] 63 p. illus. 24cm. (Beginner Books. B-28)
I. Berenstain, Janice, joint author. II. Title.
PZ8.3.B4493Bi 62-15115
ISBN: 0-394-80028-1 (trade) — ISBN: 0-394-90028-6 (lib. bdg.)
Printed in the United States of America
57 56 55 54
BEGINNER BOOKS, RANDOM HOUSE, and the Random House colophon
are registered trademarks of Random House, Inc.
THE CAT IN THE HAT logo ® and © Dr. Seuss Enterprises, L.P. 1957, renewed 1986.

We ate our honey.

We ate a lot.

Now we have no honey

In our honey pot.

Go get some honey.

Go get some more.

Go get some honey

From the honey store.

4

We will go for honey.
Come on, Small Bear!
We will go for honey
And I know where.

The store . . .
She said to
Get it there!

Not at the store.
Oh, no, Small Bear.

If a bear is smart,
If a bear knows how,
He goes on a honey hunt.
Watch me now!

How do you hunt it?

How, Dad, how?

If a bear knows how,

If a bear is smart,

He looks for a bee

Right at the start.

Bees hide their honey

In trees that are hollow.

So we will find

A bee to follow.

Is that a bee?

He went, "Buzz! Buzz!"

He looks like a bee.

Why, yes!

He does.

B-Z-Z-Z

We will follow that bee . . .

B-Z-Z-Z

We will follow that bee . . .

12

We will follow that bee
To his honey tree.

That tree!

Is that a honey tree?

B-Z-Z-Z

It looks like one
So I know it's one.
Sit down, Small Bear,
And watch the fun.
Small Bear, you watch
Your smart old Dad
Take out more honey
Than you ever had.

B-Z-Z-Z

Are you getting honey?

Are you getting a lot?

Will we take home honey

In our honey pot?

B-Z-Z-Z

That is not
A honey bee!
That was not
A honey tree.

B-Z-Z-Z

18

B-z-z-z

The bee!
The bee!
There goes the bee!

On with the honey hunt!
Follow your Pop.
Your Pop will find honey
At the very next stop.

We will follow, and follow . . .

And follow along!

I will find a new tree
And I won't be wrong.

Is that a honey tree?

How do you know?

Well, it looks just so.

And it feels just so.

Looks so. Feels so.

So it's SO!

Now watch, Small Bear.

I am about

To take that

Good old honey out.

25

How are you doing?

Are you getting a lot?

Are you getting much honey?

Or are you not?

BZ-Z-Z

Wrong kind of tree!
Wrong kind of tree!

Look, Dad!
There goes
Your friend the bee!

29

On with the hunt!
I will not rest.
I will follow that bee
To his honey nest!

When a bear is smart,
When a bear is clever,
He never gives up.
And I won't, ever!

31

B-Z-Z-Z

Dad!
Is that
A bee tree there?

33

34

I know it is.

Why, yes, Small Bear.

It can't be wrong

Like the last tree was.

Only a bee tree

Goes, "Buzz! Buzz!"

Are you getting honey?
Are you doing well?
Or is something wrong?
I smell a smell.

B-Z-Z

37

Wrong kind of tree!
Wrong kind of tree!

The bee!

The bee!

I see the bee!

B-Z-Z-Z-Z

If you want to get honey,
There is just one way.
You must follow your bee
If it takes all day.

If a bear is smart,
If a bear is bright,
A bear keeps going
If it takes all night.

B-Z-Z-Z

He went in there!
Your friend the bee!
He went in there!
Is this our tree?

Now let me think.

Now let me see . . .

This looks just like

A honey tree.

And . . .
It feels
Just like
A honey tree.

And . . .

It goes, "Buzz! Buzz!"

Like a honey tree.

47

B-Z-Z-Z

B-Z-Z-Z

And . . .
It tastes
Just like
A honey tree!
And so
You see
This tree must be—
Must, must, must be
A honey tree!

Z-Z-Z . . .

49

I never saw
More honey! Never!
Now don't you think
Your Dad is clever?

I think you are
Very clever, Dad.
But your friends the bees
Are very mad!

But Dad!
You left
The honey there!

It was not
The kind I want,
Small Bear.

I will get you honey.
I said I would.
But that bee's honey
Was not too good.

Where are you going
To find the honey?
Here in the water?
Now that seems funny.

No, we won't find honey
In here, Small Bear.
But soon, very soon
I will show you where.
When the bees have gone,
We will get along, too.
Your Dad is smart,
And he knows what to do.

But how will you
Do it, Dad?
How, Dad? How?

The best sort of honey
Never comes from bees.
It comes from a store.
I would like some,
Please.

Stan & Jan Berenstain

began writing and illustrating books for children in the early 1960s, when their two young sons, Michael and Leo, were beginning to read. They live on a hillside in Bucks County, Pennsylvania, a place that looks a lot like Bear Country. They see deer, wild turkeys, rabbits, squirrels, and woodchucks through their studio window almost every day—but no bears. The Bears live inside their hearts and minds.

The Berenstains' sons are all grown up now. Michael is an illustrator. Leo is a writer. Stan and Jan have four grandchildren. One of them can already draw pretty good bears. With more than two hundred books in print, along with videos, television shows, and even Berenstain Bears attractions at major amusement parks, it's hard to tell where the Bears end and the Berenstains begin!